HEDGEHOG HOTEL

Written by: Patricia Smith

Illustrated by: Meg Dobson-Armstrong

Cara

Hoggy hugs!

Patricia x x x

This story is dedicated to Andrea Wiseman who helped to give it life.

Special thanks goes to Nate and Louis Brown and Sian Coulson for reading the manuscript and giving their input to help make the story what it is now.

Table of Contents

HEDGEHOG HOTEL

The following stories about these hedgehogs are real and the events actually took place... Honest!

Welcome to the 'Hedgehog Hotel'

'Hedgehog Hotel'. That is what everyone called our home. "There must be a sign," they would laugh, "it says Hedgehog Hotel, except you can't see it. Hedgehogs can see it, but humans can't."

'Hedgehog Hotel' was the sign only seen by hedgehogs above the doors at No. 2 Honey Bee Street. This was the home where they knew they would be cared for; this was the home where they knew they would be loved; and unlike other hotels, they also knew they would not have to pay...!

Big ones, little ones, hungry ones, sick ones, but mostly cold ones came to stay until the weather warmed up or they felt well enough to return to the wild.

Apart from the sign only seen by hedgehogs, there is nothing special about

1

No. 2 Honey Bee Street. It is just a regular house, in a regular row of regular houses, in a regular street.

The most beautiful feature, in the small front garden, outside of the house is a large, weeping blossom tree, planted not long after we moved in, about twenty-five years ago. Long branches, dripping down like a timber waterfall, are dotted with leaves instead of fish. Thick at the trunk, they gradually thin to spindly tips which tumble to grass level and, in early spring, are adorned with the most beautiful clusters of baby-pink, cotton wool balls of flowers – making it the most stunning tree in the street for two weeks of the year.

The only other foliage in the garden, apart from the tree, are a line of bushes hugging a small wall running diagonal to the house.

Apart from our garden and the one opposite, the rest of the gardens on the estate are open plan. This means that all the other front gardens flow freely into each other with only the drives separating one property from another.

This type of layout is perfect for hedgehogs as there are very few barriers to stop them moving around. The sort of things that can restrict the movement of hedgehogs are fences, which are close to the ground and have no gap cut in a plank or have no way under. This can limit the amount of food they can find and therefore discourages them from visiting your garden.

The bushes in the front garden of No. 2 Honey Bee Street are a little overgrown. Leaves and twigs litter the base and in the winter, if it snows, the canopy is so dense, the ground remains dry. This makes it perfect for hedgehogs who want to use it to hibernate or even to simply sleep under during the day.

Around the back, the garden is a little bit bigger, although not large by any standards but, unlike the front, there is something special that might influence hedgehogs to come and stay.

Three little houses, nestled discreetly in the bushes and conifers, had 'welcome, hedgehogs' written all over them. A small tunnel, just big enough for the hogs to pass through – even the well-fed ones released in spring – led down a channel which turned into a bedding area stuffed with warm straw. A sturdy roof covered in protective rainproof material and insulating wooden walls were all that was needed to finish the perfect man-made, hedgehog house.

There are three humans that live at No. 2 Honey Bee Street: ten-year-old Joshua, me and my husband Darryl, along with two female tortoiseshell cats called Jesse and Lucy.

Darryl, Joshua and I were always rescuing animals in one form or another, but we all had to agree the most bizarre rescue of them all was when I picked up a seagull when I was cycling to work one day.

It happened not very far from home when I saw the bird sitting on a small strip of grass that ran along the side of the road. It soon became apparent something was wrong when I drew close and the seagull made no attempt to move. I stopped and wheeled my bike onto a grassy bank, then approached on foot.

Again, it did not move until I was so close, I could almost touch it. It was then that it fluttered off, but only when it was necessary. Even then it never really left the ground and stopped just a few feet away.

I quickly discovered that this was now normal for this seagull, as I chased it around the embankment, trying to round it up.

It could flap its wings, but could not take off and fluttered along just a few inches off the ground, trying to escape.

After several attempts, I finally managed to round it up and stuffed it under my right arm to carry it home. It was then that I realised I had the problem of what to do with my bike. I pondered a while before deciding the only thing I could do was to push my bicycle home with one hand and to hold on to the seagull with the other. Unfortunately, this very quickly went wrong – as it was then that the seagull decided to start a fight.

Now, we are not talking about a small seagull here, we are talking about one of those big flying pterodactyl sorts. It grabbed my neck and pulled. It pulled and twisted, its sharp beak all the while threatening to puncture my skin.

I started to panic. Desperate to get the bird off, I stretched my head away from its beak. Briefly, I succeeded, only for the seagull to have another go. It was then I knew I had to abandon my hopes of getting my bike and the bird home without help – so I called my dad.

Fortunately, he was used to being asked to take part in all sorts of weird rescue missions and was not in the least bit surprised to be asked to pick up a seagull and take it to the vets.

Fifteen minutes later, my father arrived, cat box in hand, and whisked the seagull safely off for some much-needed tender loving care.

This disastrous episode never put any of us off from rescuing any animals that came into our lives and needed help.

It is usually Darryl who finds most of the hedgehogs, often on one of his late-night walks when he gets restless in the evening. It would be then he would come back with a small hedgehog that had been hanging around outside of the Hedgehog Hotel, waiting to be noticed.

This was how it would usually happen. They would stand there, out in the open either in the back or front garden, waiting for one of the residents to see them. They had obviously seen the sign or had been told about us by their mothers or other hedgehogs they had met on their travels. Either way, this is how it came to be said,

"There's a sign above your house. 'Hedgehog Hotel'. They can definitely see it!"

Darryl did not always come home with a hedgehog, but when he did it would usually be in autumn – just when it was getting dark around about five and the days were starting to turn really cold.

Hedgehogs usually have two litters of babies, which can often contain anything from two to five hoglets.

The first litter, born around about May, will have enough time to put on the six hundred grams needed to safely hibernate through the winter.

The second litter, born around about September, can struggle to put on enough weight, especially if the weather turns cold early in autumn. These are the ones that will often not survive. These are the ones that need our help and are better off taking up residency in the Hedgehog Hotel than going it alone in the wild.

Early autumn is often when Darryl would find them after one of his walks or when he was coming back from his job working the late shift. Late season babies, too tiny to hibernate, wandering around desperately looking for food that is no longer there. And, as hedgehogs only come out after dark unless they are poorly, he would usually arrive home to find I had gone to bed...

Bedroom Shenanigans

Mid-November, soon after a cold spell arrived at the Hedgehog Hotel, Darryl found our first resident that year.

Overnight the temperature had dropped to below zero and we woke the next day to glistening bright sunshine and a sprinkling of icy diamonds on the houses, trees and grass. It was a freezing start to the day, but that night it got worse when the thermostat dropped even further.

I braced myself when I heard Darryl coming up the stairs. I always knew the way that he walked that something was wrong – he was carrying something, I could always tell. Sure enough, he came straight to the bedroom and after only a very brief warning to shield my eyes, he switched on the light.

I blinked rapidly, my pupils struggling to adjust to the sudden, painful brightness.

He hurried across the room, carrying something cupped in his hands.

He stopped at the edge of the bed and thrust a tiny spiked creature towards me. "Look!" he exclaimed. "A baby hedgehog."

The little animal, completely unafraid, pushed a small black, juicy wet nose in my direction and beamed, *'Oh, hello!'*

'Oh no...,' I groaned silently. 'There's another hedgehog on the bed.'

There had been various animals on the bed at one point or other and we are not just talking about the animals that lived in the house. Over the years these had included a couple of rabbits, a few mice, a pigeon, a homeless cat that went to live with my brother Mark, and, of course, several hedgehogs.

After a short spell on the bed and a brief introduction, our first little hedgehog was given temporary accommodation at the 'Hedgehog Hotel' that cold mid-November night.

The following day she met the third member of the household.

"Joshua!"

Joshua hurried outside when he heard Darryl call.

"Do you want to help me prepare the cage for the baby hedgehog?"

"Yes, please," he beamed.

Darryl spread some newspapers on the bottom of the large guinea pig cage whilst Joshua pulled some blankets from a box on a shelf in the garage. He opened them out, then carefully folded them ready for our latest little guest.

"Have you thought about a name?" Darryl asked.

Joshua paused a moment. "Yes. I think we should call her Poppy."

Darryl smiled. "Well it is mid-November after all. It sounds like a good name to me."

A few days later another little hedgehog, which Joshua called Holly, was also found in the front garden after another one of Darryl's walks, and not long after, a third hedgehog, which we called Apple, was found in the back garden of No. 2 Honey Bee Street.

At this point, the Hedgehog Hotel was in full swing for the winter – except for one little problem.

Joshua popped his head around the front door, his hands cupped beneath Apple's tummy. "Dad," he called. "What are we going to do?"

Darryl hurried outside to find Joshua had moved into the garage.

The garage was where the guinea pig cages were kept. A large guinea pig cage was just the right size to allow a hedgehog to have blankets at one side and a selection of food and a water dish at the other. Despite this, no matter how clean and tidy we left the cages every night, they were always in an awful mess in the morning.

The newspaper lining the floor would be dug up, wet and littered with little black torpedo-shaped droppings, or worse if they had a bout of diarrhoea. The water dish had sometimes been tipped over, soaking the floor, but even if this had not happened it would always be dirty, as they would often rinse out their mouth, swilling the food from around their teeth, and a good foot wash was obviously needed before bed. So, the bigger the cage the more chance you had to at least keep the blankets dry.

"What's wrong?" Darryl asked.

"We only have two guinea pig cages and we now have three hedgehogs but, as there is no more room for more guinea pig cages in the garage, we need to come up with a solution."

"Oh, I see what you mean." Darryl thought a moment. "The bottom cage is slightly bigger than the top one, so we could split that one in half and put two hedgehogs in the same cage on either side of the separation. The only problem with that is that each side might be a little bit too small for the hedgehogs." He began to re-shuffle the cages to see if his plan would work.

Joshua waited, continuing to hold the hedgehog, his fingers around her warm belly where there was soft fur rather than spines. "Hello, Apple," he said, smiling at the little creature as she tried to consider whether he was a threat or not and whether she needed to curl up.

Apple's nose came out, then just as quickly tucked in again, her eyes sinking and the spines on her forehead shooting forward.

'Hurf! Hurf! See my spines, you can't hurt me.'

Suddenly Joshua had a thought. "Apple feels like she is bigger than the other two and she was found in a different location."

Darryl stopped. "And?"

"Holly and Poppy were found in the front garden and they're both about the same size. Do you think they might be sisters?"

"They could be. What's your point?"

"Do you think we could try putting them together in the same cage and see if they get along?"

"The same cage without something to separate them?"

"Yes."

Darryl raised his eyebrows. "It's certainly worth a try."

A short while later after a quick bedding reshuffle, Holly and Poppy were both moved to the same enclosure.

Food and water, enough for two, was placed in the middle and at the farthest points, on opposite sides were the blankets, each containing one small female hedgehog. Except it did not stay that way for long, as almost immediately, Holly vacated her blanket and rushed across the cage to snuggle into bed with Poppy.

Joshua smiled. "Aah... How cute. She obviously wants to be with her sister."

The new system for bedding the hedgehogs seemed to go well. Every morning Holly would be snuggled up with Poppy, either directly next to her or wrapped up in a different layer of the same blanket. This went on for just over a week until one day, when the two hedgehogs were in the small collapsible puppy run, used to keep them safe whilst they were being cleaned out, Joshua noticed there was a bit of shoving and snorting going on between the pair. "Come and look at this," he called. "They definitely seem to be unhappy with each other about something."

I stood over the puppy run, looking down at the squabbling that was taking place. "Yes, you're right," I said.

"Do you think one of them started it?" Joshua asked, concerned.

"I'm not sure, but as Poppy is the bigger one and seems to be doing most of the shoving, there's a chance it could be her."

Moments later Darryl came in, his head turned away, his arms filled with dirty blankets.

"What?" I said in dismay. "They need changing again already." I took the smelly bundle, turned my face away from the stench and headed straight for the washing machine. "I thought you said these hedgehogs were clean."

Over the years, the household had been host to lots of hedgehogs ranging from the very clean, who came out of their beds and toileted in one particular corner, to the ones whose beds were dirty by the time you walked two paces away from the cage.

"Poppy used to be clean, but her standards seem to have suddenly dropped," he called, "and she's now pooing in her blankets."

"Oh, lovely," I said sarcastically. "I'll make sure I check these thoroughly before I put them through the machine."

Joshua brought Darryl up to date on the activities of the hedgehogs and it was decided that they should try to let Holly sleep in the same cage as Apple to see if that worked better.

There was another quick bedding re-shuffle and much to Joshua and Darryl's surprise, Holly did exactly the same thing that she did when she was put in with Poppy.

Her bedding was at the far side of the cage, but Holly seemed unhappy with this and she charged out of her blankets and snuggled up with Apple.

"That seems to be going well," Darryl beamed. "Hopefully, they'll be alright."

They left the garage, pulled down the door and secured it for the night.

The following day, though, all was not well...

Holly's blanket remained untouched and it was obvious that it had not been slept in at all.

Apple's fleeces, on the other hand, looked like they had been dragged through the mud then dumped in an untidy heap, roughly where they had been left the previous night.

"What on Earth has happened," Darryl said, bemused when he saw the state of the blankets, as Apple had also been particularly clean and tidy until now. Quickly he rummaged through the bedding and confirmed both hedgehogs were in the same fleece, but in different folds, as far away from each other as possible. "Come on, let's get them cleaned out," he sighed.

Darryl set up the puppy run whilst Joshua removed the two hedgehogs from the cage. He put them into the enclosure and was shocked to see within seconds they were shoving and snorting at each other in the same way that Poppy and Holly had done the previous day.

I stepped into the room, just as the pair began jostling.

"What do you think could be wrong?" Joshua asked.

I looked into the run. "They don't seem to be very happy with each other."

"I think I know what could be the problem," Darryl called from the doorway. He came into the room, carrying the ruined fleeces. He placed them on the floor then opened them up to reveal a dirty pile in the centre of a dip. "Nobody wants to sleep with Holly because she poops in her blankets."

"Are you sure it's Holly?" I asked.

"Yes. Both of the other hedgehogs were very clean until Holly started to sleep with them."

"Then the solution would be to put Apple and Poppy together," Joshua said, "and to give Holly a bed all of her own."

It was decided that this was a good plan and after one more bedding re-shuffle everyone was settled into their new accommodation.

Apple and Poppy were content; they respected each other's space and stayed in their own beds, whilst Holly, who needed her covers changing a lot more than the others, could poop in her own blankets to her heart's content without anyone complaining.

That should have been that and everyone should have been happy – but somehow still the situation was not perfect.

A week later Joshua stepped into the garage and looked in dismay at a nearly full dish of food on the floor of one of the guinea pig cages. "Holly doesn't seem to be eating very much," he said, concerned, "and it's been getting worse for the last few days."

I looked at the bowl of barely touched dried maggots and cat food. "You're right. Let's weigh her and see if she is any lighter."

Sure enough, Holly had lost fifty grams, which was a lot for a creature which would usually only weigh not much more than eight hundred grams at its heaviest.

"What are we going to do?" Joshua asked. "She was eating quite happily when she shared a bed with the other hedgehogs, but neither one of them want her there because she dirties the blankets."

"She's obviously miserable on her own," I added. "We do have quite a dilemma."

The next day I discussed the Holly problem at work and my friend Catriona came up with a brilliant solution!

We got Holly a teddy so that she did not feel alone and, to our delight, suddenly she started eating again.

Joshua looked into the cage and smiled. "She's got someone she can snuggle up to, who won't complain or argue back and does not protest or shove her around – even if she does poo the bed."

The bedding arrangement continued to go well and in early spring all three hedgehogs were released in the dark, within an hour of each other.

"Stay safe, babies," I muttered as I hurried to the house.

Holly with her teddy.

The Diary of a Bald Hedgehog

Week One

Darryl rushed into the house. He had been on one of his walks and came back looking more than a little bit flustered. It was early, rather than late evening, so the whole household was still up.

"You won't believe what I've just seen," he announced to no one in particular in the room. "A little bald hedgehog."

Joshua had been watching television. He twisted around so that he could see his dad better. "A bald hedgehog?" he said questioningly, convinced he had heard wrong.

"Yes, a bald hedgehog," Darryl repeated.

"Are you sure it was a hedgehog and not a rat?" I asked.

"Yes, I am. It had no tail. It was definitely a hedgehog."

"Where is it?" Joshua asked. "A bald hedgehog wouldn't be able to protect itself and would be easy prey for a predator."

"It must also be very poorly if it's lost all of its spines," I added.

"It ran away and disappeared into the bushes before I got the chance to round it up."

"Well, there's nothing you can do if you can't find it," I said. "But you will have to keep an eye out for it and try to catch it over the next few days, as it will be vulnerable."

A couple of nights later Darryl finally managed to capture the little bald hedgehog, very close to the Hedgehog Hotel, and brought it home with him from his walk.

"That sprint was not an extraordinary burst of speed for this little one and I nearly lost it again," he informed us as we gathered in a curious huddle to stare at the spineless hedgehog.

"It's not completely bald," Darryl said, tipping the hedgehog back so that its tummy was exposed.

This movement was enough to make the little animal nervous and triggered a series of head dips in a fruitless attempt to activate spines that were not there and protect itself from an attack that was not happening.

Darryl lifted the hedgehog higher so that its underside could be seen. "It does have a thin skirt of fur around its sides, where the base of the spines would have been." He manoeuvred the hedgehog so that it was closer to the light. "What is it? A boy or a girl?"

"There is a bump in the middle of a very bald tummy," I informed him, "therefore it's a boy."

"He doesn't look like a hedgehog at all without his spines," Joshua laughed. "His head looks like it belongs to a rat, but his body makes him look more like a tiny armadillo."

"He does that," I chuckled, "or maybe an anteater or an aardvark. Definitely something beginning with 'A'," I called as I left the room. "I'll get him some food." I headed for the kitchen with Darryl and Joshua immediately behind.

I prepared a plate of cat food, shooed Lucy off as she had already been fed several times that day and stepped back whilst Darryl put the little hedgehog down in front of the dish.

Immediately the poor little creature started eating. Huge mouthfuls were devoured as though he had not eaten for days. This went on for some time with only a couple of brief pauses to check that we, plus one cat, were not going to launch an attack when he was not looking. Still despite this, it was almost as though he did not care if he died, just as long as he could get one more mouthful of food down, before he was killed. It seemed as if he could not get the food down fast enough and when the dish was empty, I filled it again. By now he seemed to have realised he was safe and did not flinch or even pause when I scooped the remaining contents of the tin out onto the plate.

A dish and a half of cat food later, the hedgehog was slowing down.

"I'm surprised it can still breathe," I said, "there can't be much room left for the lungs. Have you thought of a name?" I asked Joshua.

"I think it will have to be Horace because he's definitely a hungry one."

"Hungry Horace," I laughed. "It's very fitting."

Horace was the only hedgehog to stay at the Hedgehog Hotel that year and, as he was so bald and had virtually nothing to keep him warm, he was honoured enough to stay in the 'Special Guest' room inside the house.

The first night he slept in a large plastic box, usually used to store blankets, with two small dishes at one end, one for food and the other for water, and at the other end was a fleece to keep him warm.

The following morning Joshua rose early. He went in to check on our little guest and stopped in the doorway, his mouth open, shocked to be confronted by the devastation of poo.

The cat food was all gone and the small dish, which had originally held meat, now contained a neat pile of hedgehog droppings. He had also dirtied in his blanket and trodden it all over the bottom of the box.

Joshua gaped at the wreckage in horror.

Darryl came into the room and looked at the carnage. "I don't think he has enough space. That'll be the problem."

"We could maybe get one of the guinea pig cages from the garage and bring it upstairs," Joshua suggested.

"Yes," Darryl said. "That's a good idea."

Horace's sleeping arrangements were changed by Darryl whilst Joshua and I took him to the vets to get a better idea of why he lost his spines.

The journey in the car gave Horace an opportunity to display more of his personality.

Joshua sat in the front, a small box on his knee, with a very alert hedgehog standing on top of his blankets, in the middle of the container. "I've never seen a hedgehog do that before," he said.

"What is he doing?" I asked.

"He's not hiding under his blanket in the way they usually do. He's standing in the middle of his box with his body quite high off the ground, trying his best to look around."

I turned the car into the vets' and pulled into a parking space before I peeked inside the box. "He's a proper little character," I said, smiling.

The vet confirmed Horace had ringworm and we returned home with a bottle of medicine and instructions for treatment, which would take place over the next few weeks to help him get better.

Week Two

Joshua came home from school and put his bag down by the door. Briefly, he looked up the stairs before he came into the kitchen. "What's the laughter about upstairs?"

"I'm not sure," I replied. "Your dad is seeing to Horace. Why don't you pop up and see what's going on."

He left the room and trotted up the stairs. As he neared the landing he could hear talking coming from the 'Special Guest' room. He opened the door and found Darryl cleaning out Horace's cage. "What's funny?" Joshua asked.

"Horace is obviously feeling a bit better now that he's grown a few of his spines

38

back and he can sprint even faster than ever." Darryl stood. "He's so keen to get into his blankets before I even get them sorted that no matter how far from the bedding area I put them, he manages to dash in before I can fold them properly. Also, look at this." Darryl took a step back and Joshua saw a small lump moving around beneath a sheet of newspaper.

"He's into everything," Darryl continued. "I can't put anything down fast enough before he's there, wanting to get involved." He lifted the newspaper up to reveal the little hedgehog, who was still mostly, but not entirely, bald. "Can you get a box to put him in, otherwise it's going to take forever to clean him out?"

A couple of weeks into his treatment, a few spines had begun to emerge around the top of Horace's head and shoulders and although there was not enough for him to be able to protect himself, he did at least look a little bit more like a hedgehog.

Preparing the cage was much easier without Horace's 'help' and soon he was in, sorted and comfortable, and tucking into his third meal of the day.

Horace's meal times had become a source of delight for the family and we regularly gathered to watch the little hedgehog eat.

'Squeak, squeak.'

"He makes the sweetest little noises when he drinks," Joshua said.

"He so loves his food," Darryl added.

Horace finished his cat food on one plate and turned his attention to another. He snuffled around, briefly sniffing at the contents, unimpressed with what was on offer before starting to shove the dish away with the bridge of his nose. *'Take it away, woman. Take it away.'*

"Yes, he does like his food," I said, "but he makes it quite clear if he doesn't want something." Quickly, I moved the dish before he tipped it over.

"I popped into the room last night on the way to the bathroom," Joshua said. "His blanket was twitching and he was making the strangest noises. I went to see what was going on and when I pulled back the fleece, I found him snoring and having a very animated dream," he laughed, "legs twitching and everything. He was obviously off on a very exciting adventure."

Week Three

After a few weeks, Horace had really started to appreciate his fleeces and it was difficult for anyone cleaning him out to get the blankets sorted before he was there, demanding to be in and wrapped up in the soft warmth. We were taking it in turns to clean him out as he was so messy it had to be done twice a day, sometimes more.

It was my turn one evening and I had emptied the cage of everything except Horace. I was preparing the newspapers and blankets when I suddenly noticed him moving around his enclosure in a strange manner. He was pacing backwards and forwards from one side of the container to the other, running his chin along the bottom of the box.

"He wants to be under something."

I jumped when Joshua spoke to me from behind. I looked around. "I've never seen him doing that before."

"He started doing it a couple of days ago," he said. "He's a clever hedgehog and very good at communicating his feelings."

Quickly, I popped a blanket down and sure enough, within seconds Horace was beneath it.

Cleaning him out from then on always had to involve another box so that Horace could stay warm whilst his cage was being prepared.

It was in week three that we decided to start giving Horace cat crunchies to keep his jaws and teeth strong, as he would need to be able to crunch snails and beetles when he returned to the wild.

This little project started out well and Horace embraced his new diet with relish.

Then one day, towards the end of the week, Darryl reported there had been a terrifying incident when Horace was happily making his way through a small dish of biscuits.

Suddenly, his little body began to jerk and as Darryl looked on with growing concern, the hedgehog began to back away and wipe the side of his mouth. It was then, Darryl told us, he realised to his horror that Horace was choking. 'What am I going to do?' he thought in a panic.

Quickly, he opened the cage and was just about to try to hang him upside down to dislodge the biscuit, when suddenly Horace coughed it up. It landed at Horace's feet and immediately he recovered. *'Oh, food!'* Out shot his tongue and he scoffed the soggy biscuit down, properly this time.

From that point on, it was decided, Horace should not be left alone when eating crunchies.

Week Four

To increase his healing, part of Horace's daily routine included a brush with a child's soft toothbrush.

This helped to remove the dead skin and improved his overall appearance.

He seemed, at first, to thoroughly dislike this and although he never curled up, he would snort loudly and thrust his head upward in an attempt to shove whoever was brushing him off.

At one point, Joshua said, "He became so agitated he actually left the ground and jumped up with a loud snort, making it quite clear that he wanted me to stop."

After a while Horace learned to tolerate most areas of his body being brushed, even the side of his face, but he never got used to the back of his neck being touched and would protest vigorously if this area was ever brushed.

It was the first weekend of the fourth week that Horace had been with us when there was a sudden hot spell.

Horace had come to the Hedgehog Hotel in May and would not have usually taken up residency, due to his size, if it had not been for his lack of spines. So, as time went on it was the warmer weather not the cold that became a problem.

The Sunday was particularly hot. I went upstairs, early in the evening, to clean out and feed Horace, and was alarmed to find the room uncomfortably warm.

The house is east-west facing so the front gets the sun in the morning and the back gets it afternoon onwards. It had been a very hot day, so the whole house was already warm by the time the sun hit the back bedroom window late afternoon.

Quickly, I checked on Horace as he had been lying in the full glare of the beams pouring through the glass.

His instincts, to hide, had only added to the problem and as I pulled back the fleeces, I was shocked to find his belly sweaty and he felt like a hot potato when I touched his little body.

Rather ironically, he looked like a little potato as well, except one with a snout and legs.

Slowly he emerged from the blanket in a wobbly state.

'My eyes are too hot, one of my back legs doesn't work properly and I might just fall over.'

Despite this, it was still, *'Oh, food,'* when I placed down the plate.

"Could somebody bring a fan?" I called downstairs.

Briefly, I heard scrambling in a cupboard before Joshua rushed upstairs carrying a small desk fan.

We set it on a chair and a short while later Horace looked considerably better after a good slurp of water and a spell of cooling.

"Why don't we cover one half of the guinea pig cage with a blanket to make sure it's shaded so that he doesn't overheat again," Joshua suggested.

I brightened. "That's a good idea. We might have to move him around, but I'm sure that won't matter."

Horace and his bedding were transferred to the opposite side of the cage and a blanket was placed over the bars to provide additional shade before we left him to settle down for the night.

The next morning Joshua went in early to check on Horace, before he went to school, but before long the entire family were in the bedroom when he called us into the room.

"What's wrong?" I asked.

Joshua beamed. "It looks like he wasn't very happy about his bedding being moved to the other side of the cage. He seems to have spent the night trying to put things back to the way they were."

We looked into the cage and saw that the only things that had prevented Horace from carrying out a complete furniture reshuffle had been his dishes on the far end of the enclosure.

Food was caked across his blankets where he had attempted to drag them to the opposite side, or the original in his opinion, and they were half soaked with water.

We cleaned him out and as the weather had turned cooler, put him back to where he had obviously been more comfortable.

Over the next few weeks, we were to get used to the furniture being reshuffled, as it was to become an occasional night-time pastime, no matter where we left his blankets.

Week Five

In week five another trip to the vets confirmed the ringworm had cleared up and it was suggested it might be a good idea to start getting Horace used to the outside world again.

"Do you think we should just put him outside in a box," Joshua asked, when we returned home, "to get him used to the temperature and smells of the garden again?"

"That would be a good start, but I don't think it will help him to get his strength back," I said. "He needs to move around for that."

Joshua bent down and stroked Jesse, who had just come into the kitchen, hoping to get an early tea. Then suddenly he stood, a look of amusement lighting his face. "How about we try Horace outside with a kitten harness. That way he can walk around the garden, but we'll be able to stop him running away, certainly until his spines have grown fully back."

I smiled. "I like it. It's certainly worth a try."

The following day I picked up a kitten harness on my way home from work and that weekend the whole family, including the cats, gathered to take Horace on his first walk in the garden.

"I think it might be too big," Darryl said. He fiddled with the harness, then bent to try it on the hog and was surprised to find it was quite the opposite and instead it needed slackening a little.

Darryl had the dubious honour of 'dressing' Horace. He expected a battle and at least a few head dips as he attached the harness but, instead, much to his relief, Horace seemed completely unafraid and remained co-operative throughout the hooking up process. The only time he jumped slightly was when the catch around his neck was snapped into place. Darryl stood and smiled. "So far so good." He picked up Horace and the rest of the family followed him outside.

To our absolute delight Horace paid no heed to the harness.

Whoosh! He was off. And seemed to love it. Nose down, sniffing like a steam train every step of the way, he led Darryl to the bottom of the garden, where he immediately started digging up insects and worms.

He raked in the soil and was suddenly crunching, then turned over a leaf and was at it again. For a creature with such apparently poor eyesight, he was an amazing hunter of the small and minute due to his fantastic sense of smell. Tiny insects, that we could barely see, were uncovered and devoured in a flash.

Half an hour later, Horace was still full of life.

Joshua took over the lead, but its length was short so he had to keep lifting the little hog back onto the grass every time he wandered into some bushes.

Still, Horace did not seem to mind and nothing appeared to faze him – not even the wet grass, which drenched his short, bare legs and exposed stomach.

Joshua stayed behind, his arm outstretched, holding the lead at its full length, far enough away to make sure he did not risk standing on Horace, but close enough to be able to step quickly in if the little hog should get into trouble.

Horace headed for the compost bin. It seemed to hold many delights and he took a great deal of time investigating the area surrounding the base. Some fluid had oozed from the bottom and as the little hog drew near, Joshua picked him up and moved him around it to stop him walking through the liquid. Not long after, he got tangled in a bush and it was then we decided it was time to return him indoors.

The harness snapped off even easier than it snapped on and once again, Horace stood patiently waiting for Joshua to carefully remove it.

I returned Horace back to his cage.

Joshua popped into the 'Special Guest' room on his way to bed. "How is he doing?"

"He seems completely happy and his appetite is even more ferocious than usual."

"What?" Joshua laughed. "Despite all the bugs he ate."

I placed a clean blanket in Horace's cage and closed the lid, ready to leave him for the night.

"Wait for it..." Joshua smiled. "Wait for the mad dash." Then his face fell when to our surprise, it never came.

Horace seemed happy to stay outside of his blankets and wandered around the cage completely alert.

"Well there's a first," I said. "Come on, we'll leave him to it. He'll put himself to bed when he's ready."

Half an hour later, I popped my head in the door and saw he had settled, but his new-found energy became a problem later that night.

It was about two in the morning that we woke to hear scraping noises coming from the 'Special Guest' room.

Darryl and I rose, went next door and were horrified when we clicked the light on to find the little hog had completely wrecked his cage.

Standing in the middle of the decimation was Horace, holding himself up, high off the ground in the same way he had when he was off to the vets, looking very defiant.

'I'm a big boy now, so what are you going to do about it?'

All the newspapers were dug up and had been piled at one end of his cage and his drenched fleece was on the other.

We looked at each other, unsure of whether to laugh or cry.

"He's got nowhere to sleep; we'll have to change him," Darryl said.

I looked at the mess, exasperated. "I'm not even sure where to start."

"You get the clean blankets and newspapers and I'll clear out the dirty cage. Before you know it, between the two of us, we'll have it all done."

Ten minutes later we crawled back into bed, leaving Horace, now exhausted after enough excitement for one night, happily settled into a clean dry fleece – and thankfully he stayed that way for the rest of the night.

Week Eight

Every day Horace had a spell in the garden before bedtime. It was on one of these trips when Joshua and I had been outside for only a short time that we realised we had an audience.

It was Joshua who noticed first. He looked around to see Lucy and Jesse sat by the car. Further down the drive two more cats that lived in the street had also arrived to watch the show and finally, two strays that were fed by the locals settled at the bottom of the garden.

"Look at this lot," he said in a hushed voice.

I looked around to see all of the cats ignoring each other and animals that would usually squabble, most notably Lucy who seemed to fight with everyone, sat side by side, all eyes trained on Horace.

They were fascinated by him and even, I would say, a little afraid. No one came close and their eyes never strayed from his every move. Six heads swivelled in his direction as they wondered, *'What on earth is that little goblin doing on a lead?'*

This continued, much to our amusement, until the show broke up twenty minutes later when we took him inside.

The following evening Darryl returned Horace to the back garden for his nightly exercise and it was then that he became

Horrible Horace, when he discovered he could slip out of the harness.

"I'm going to loosen the straps slightly because I'm frightened they might hurt him now he has a few more spines," Darryl said. He moved the buckle up a little, then closed the catch before taking Horace into the garden.

It was not long before Horace was out of the harness though. Initially it seemed like he had slipped it accidentally when his front foot became caught in the collar section, which Darryl had slackened a little bit too much. The moment the limb became entangled, Horace rolled onto his side and squirmed around, attempting to release it and it was then that he managed to pull his head free.

Quickly, Darryl replaced the harness around his neck and we could have thought the next time Horace released his head was also an accident, if it had not happened twice more in the next five minutes. Each time he rolled onto his side, squirmed around and pulled his head free of the loop.

Joshua stepped outside to find Darryl tightening the collar. "What are you doing?" he asked. "I thought you wanted it loosened."

"He keeps wriggling free." Darryl said. Finished, he stood and waited for Horace to start moving around the garden again but, instead, the little hog just sat there, his nose pointing to the ground, looking to all like a right, proper little gruff.

"Come on, Horace," Darryl encouraged, tugging gently on the lead, but the hedgehog continued to refuse to move. "What's he doing?" he asked, baffled.

Joshua laughed. "He's sulking."

"Well sulking or not, he has to wear the harness."

With a little coaxing Darryl finally managed to get him moving and for a few minutes he followed the hedgehog around the garden until suddenly Horace rolled onto his side and with his foot under his chin, proceeded to try to wriggle out of the collar again. This time, though, it had just been tightened and he could not manage to release the strap enough to break free. He continued to try for a short while longer before he suddenly got upset and curled up into a ball.

Quickly, Darryl bent and released the harness, afraid he might choke.

Immediately, Horace uncurled and with a look of glee on his face, began to walk freely around the garden.

"Help me to keep an eye on him," Darryl said to Joshua, "he's obviously decided he's not prepared to tolerate the harness any more."

Despite Darryl's concerns, Horace made no attempt to run away. He was patiently guided from the bushes and even came up to sniff at Joshua's shoe.

A good half hour was spent outside until Horace wandered over to the birdbath where he stopped, no longer willing to move. It was then that they knew he was tired and it was time to go inside.

Week Nine

We became concerned when Horace suddenly started to lose the few spines he had gained.

Darryl took him back to the vets and it was then that we discovered how much weight he had lost. The last time he had been weighed he was five hundred and fifty grams; this time he was four hundred and twenty grams.

The vet was no longer concerned about his ringworm, which tests proved had completely cleared up, and they started to treat him for lungworm instead.

Hedgehogs often carry a small load of parasites in any case, but when their immune system is down, as with the ringworm, they can become overrun. If left untreated, lungworm can lead to pneumonia, bleeding of the lungs and death so it was important we made sure our little hog got the treatment. Unfortunately, Horace had been happily chomping on slugs and snails during our outings in the garden, which have been known to transmit lungworm.

Darryl returned home with another batch of medicine and Horace started more treatment that day. A creamy liquid needed to be added to his food and although it was only a small amount, it still turned out to be quite a lot of medicine to try to hide in amongst the meat and biscuits fed to him twice a day.

That night I watched as he carefully made his way around the ooze, to pick out the untainted cat meat. Without doubt, he could detect it.

It was in week nine, around the time that he started his new treatment, that Horace discovered the delights of breakfast in bed. Whoever fed him reported back that the moment the food was presented, no matter where he was in his cage, he would rush into his fleeces and wait until the plate was put under his nose before he ate, wrapped up and warm in his blankets.

Despite the treatment, the weight loss continued. Worried, we decided the best thing would be to give Horace to our local hedgehog rescue centre. We travelled up the next day and passed him over for expert care.

It was then we discovered that I was not very good at sexing hedgehogs. It turned out Horace was in fact a female. As we sadly said our goodbyes, Horace became Harriet, who, when better, was ready for release by the autumn.

Harriet eating cat food in the garden.

Harriet on her harness.

The Three Bears

The year of The Three Bears, the weather turned very cold suddenly, early in November, and the 'Hedgehog Hotel' had a rapid influx of guests when three hedgehogs came to stay pretty much one after the other.

A cold snap had brought an early snowfall that, we were to discover, would go on for quite a few months and would lead to drifts several feet deep.

As the three came in, no more than a couple of days apart over the space of a week, Joshua nicknamed them 'The Three Bears'.

There was the little one, Willow, the middle one, Lucky, and the big one, Spike.

Spike was the first to come in to the hotel, and it seemed as though our biggest arrival had definitely been told where to come.

Other hedgehogs or their mothers would say, *'If you need any help, hurt yourself or need to be looked after for the winter, this is where you go. Look out for the sign.'*

Joshua had seen Spike in the garden just as the cold spell arrived, but before it really bit. Early evening he was outside filling up the containers hanging from the apple tree in the back, when he saw Spike running along the edge of the bushes. He called me out and together we rounded the hedgehog up.

"We'll weigh him," I said. "If he's more than six hundred grams we can let him go back outside as he'll be big enough to hibernate."

Joshua popped Spike on the scales and allowed the dish to take the hedgehog's weight. "Six hundred and seventy grams," he read from the dial. He looked up, "So he should be alright."

"Good. We'll pop him out again as he might have just been checking out the dens. Are you finished filling up the feeders?"

"Yes."

"OK, leave him alone and hopefully he'll settle in the garden for the winter."

The following weekend Honey Bee Street woke to its first covering of snow. It was only a light dusting, not even enough to cover the grass, but was sufficient to make the cats reluctant to step beyond the doors.

It was Saturday afternoon, a time for cooking, shopping or relaxing with a good book. This particular Saturday, I was preparing my first batch of Christmas cakes. I went into the kitchen and looked outside and saw Spike standing in the snow, directly opposite the window as though he were waiting to be discovered.

This was made more alarming as it was still daylight and a clear indication that he wanted to come and stay in the 'Hedgehog Hotel'.

I stepped outside and picked Spike up with ease, as he made no attempt to run away this time.

A cage was prepared in the 'Special Guest' room, as it was feared that the sudden cold spell would be too much for the garage, and Spike made himself at home.

He was a nervous guest and seemed less bold than some of the other hedgehogs that had stayed at the hotel. Still, we did our best to create a calm atmosphere and not long after he arrived, he was joined by Willow.

Willow was spotted running across the snow, which, a couple of days later, was quite deep. At first, Darryl had thought she was a rat when he saw her running along the bottom of the garden. She was about the same size at the rump, but was shorter and less lean and, of course, was missing a tail –

not that he could see that much detail from the upstairs window.

He grabbed a torch and went outside to investigate.

The little hedgehog was so light, she left no footprints in the freshly fallen snow. There was no trail.

Desperate to find her, he swung the torch around the garden in the direction he had seen the hedgehog heading. After a few minutes of searching and scrambling in the snow, he was just about to give up when suddenly he spotted her running amongst the thick trunks of conifers that formed a hedge along the fence which separated our garden from the next.

Quickly, he dropped to his knees, snow soaking through his trousers, and grabbed the tiny hedgehog. A short while later, 'The

Hedgehog Hotel' had its smallest resident that year.

Willow was little enough to fit into one hand, even for Joshua. She was only about two inches long and would have been not much more than six weeks old.

"Do you think that Willow and Spike might be OK together," Joshua asked later as he helped prepare the cage for our latest resident.

"Do you want to try them?" Darryl asked.

"Yes."

Joshua was holding Willow whilst Darryl prepared newspapers and blankets for both of the cages and, as it was a good time to also clean out Spike, the larger hedgehog was in the puppy run to keep him out of the way. Joshua popped Willow down and the little hedgehog rushed over and stood beside Spike.

Darryl stopped what he was doing and looked into the run. "That seems promising. Shall we see if they'll sleep together?"

"Yes." Joshua smiled. "They might be happier and it might help to make Spike feel more comfortable."

Darryl nodded. "That's a good idea. He's definitely very nervous."

The two hedgehogs were put into the same cage with plenty of blankets to keep them warm and were left to settle down for the night.

The follow morning the family were all up early, keen to see the result of the pairing.

Joshua was first into the room.

"How did it go?" I asked, leaning around to look into the cage.

"I don't think it went very well," Joshua groaned.

Willow was sitting, looking very miserable, on top of a pile of fleecy blankets covering a large lump.

"It looks like she's been kicked out of bed," I said.

"It's just as well they weren't in the garage," Joshua stated. He opened the cage and retrieved the little hedgehog so that Darryl could check the internal occupant.

Before Willow had arrived, Spike had been our cleanest hedgehog yet. He left his bedding to go to the toilet and always used a particular corner. He never dug up the newspapers and sometimes in the morning, apart from the fact that the food was missing, you would never know he was there. But, as Darryl pulled back the blankets, he could see that Spike was also not very happy as there before us lay the devastation of poo.

Tiny torpedo-shaped black droppings littered the inside of the blanket and worst of all, there was one on the bridge of Spike's nose.

"No, this is definitely not going to work," Darryl stated.

"Come on, big one," he picked Spike up, "we'll get you cleaned up, and little one," he looked at Willow, clasped firmly in Joshua's hands, "we'll get you into your own cage."

A couple of days later we had to go back to the large plastic box, which was big enough for little Willow, when we ran out of cages when Lucky arrived.

I was moving the rubbish bin late one night as the collectors were coming the next day. As I pulled the bin around to the front of the house, there in the garden was a hedgehog – just standing, waiting to be noticed.

He never ran away. Instead, he just stood there, hoping to be seen and checked into the hotel.

I abandoned my task and quickly took the little one inside. In the kitchen, I put him down in front of a plate of food, but unlike Horace, who turned out to be Harriet, Lucky did not immediately eat. Instead, he shuffled away and hid his face in a corner, too cold to even curl up.

"Poor baby, you thought you were going to die," I said softly.

Lucky's choice of name was easy, as we knew how incredibly lucky he was.

A weather front had moved down from Siberia, freezing the snow and dropping the nightly temperatures to minus ten degrees. It had just arrived that day and if I had not found Lucky, who may have been standing in the garden for sometime waiting to be noticed, he would have surely died.

Lucky turned out to be my absolute favourite hedgehog because he had such an amazing personality – but more of that later.

I took him upstairs and decided I would have to do a little bit of a bedding shuffle as we now had three hedgehogs (The Three Bears) and only two cages.

Joshua came in and I left him watching Lucky and Willow, who had been removed from her cage to allow her to get some exercise, whilst I got a big box out of the attic.

The job complete, I returned to the bedroom in time to hear Joshua telling Willow off.

"What's wrong?"

"She's bullying Lucky."

I looked down to see the tiny hedgehog, half the size of our new arrival, ramming into the side of the bigger male.

Lucky, still too cold to react, stood there with a look on his face that was halfway between bafflement and alarm.

I put the box down and bent to pick Willow up, but before I could reach her, she shoved her nose underneath Lucky's belly and began to push for all she was worth.

She pushed and scraped, her feet slipping on the carpet in the process. She heaved and shoved and had just managed to lift him slightly off the ground when suddenly she pooed herself with the effort.

"Get off, you little thug!" I picked her up and put her into the box to keep her away from Lucky.

It was not long, though, before we realised that Willow's pooing was actually a problem when she stopped putting on weight. In a sense, it was a blessing, as a couple of days later another hedgehog came to stay at the hotel.

Boudicca, who was not found on the grounds of the hotel, came to join us in early December after one of Darryl's walks. She had been spotted running along the edge of a fence, at the top of the road, not long after dark and it was immediately obvious that she was way too small for hibernation. She could have also been called Lucky, as it was a miracle she had survived in the snow.

We now had four guests, some of whom had questionable toileting habits, which meant cleaning them out could take up to one and a half hours, twice a day.

"What are we going to do?" Darryl groaned on the second day of a mammoth clean. "This is getting out of hand."

"I could ask if my friend Jackie can take one of the hedgehogs to ease the load," I suggested.

Darryl brightened. "Could you?"

"We could give her Spike as he is such a sweetheart and exceptionally clean, with his toilet corner."

Jackie loves hedgehogs and is a member of St. Tiggywinkles, so I knew she would be an excellent carer for our largest resident. It was with great relief that she was able to take Spike, who turned out to be a female and became Skype, as again I failed to sex the hedgehog correctly.

Skype was adored and cared for beautifully by Jackie and as a result she thrived and became a lot more relaxed in a household where she was the only hedgehog.

Skype interacted with Jackie and her husband Ian in a way that she never did with us and one day, Jackie reported that there had been a little bit too much interaction with Skype when Ian had been helping to watch the hedgehog whilst she was being cleaned out.

He had been lying on the floor watching Skype whilst she ran around investigating the room and getting some exercise. She kept coming up to Ian and on a couple of occasions had even climbed over the top of his legs. Then suddenly he realised there was a problem when Skype unexpectedly made her way up his trousers. She had

moved up, far enough for the fabric to become tight, then as she was forced against his leg she began to get stressed and, as a result, curled up into a spiky ball.

Ian began to panic and tried to get her out, but every time he attempted to extract her, using gravity or otherwise, she curled up again and her spines stabbed him painfully in the leg.

Eventually, Jackie said, the only way they could get her out was to slowly and carefully lower Ian's trousers, with the hedgehog still inside.

It was not long after Jackie took on Skype that we passed Willow on to the local hedgehog rescue centre, as she was not gaining weight and we were worried about her diarrhoea.

Thankfully that took us from four to a much more manageable two hedgehogs – Lucky and Boudicca.

Lucky's personality very quickly began to emerge and was demonstrated, in particular, when he was being cleaned out. He proved himself to be very clever and soon learned how the door to the 'Special Guest' room opened.

"You have to be careful when you go into the room," Joshua warned me one day when I came upstairs carrying clean plates and found him scrambling in the study next door, chasing after Lucky with a blanket.

"I take it he got out?" I questioned.

"Yes. He waits by the door at the point where it opens and rushes out as fast as he can the moment he gets the opportunity."

"Why do you have the blanket?"

Joshua looked up. He had cornered Lucky by the bookcase. "He seems to be determined to get into the study. It's like he has to be in there, simply because he's not allowed."

The moment Joshua approached, Lucky instantly curled into a tight ball of spines in an attempt to stop himself being picked up.

"Oh, I see why you need the blanket," I said.

As Joshua lowered the fleece, Lucky pulled himself into a tighter ball.

'No! Don't take me out of this room. I want to look around.'

Joshua picked the hedgehog up and returned him to the 'Special Guest' room.

The moment he was unravelled Lucky was off, his spiky mood forgotten, running around the room, his nose sniffing everywhere like a little steam train.

Darryl was in the room, kneeling on the floor, cleaning out the cages when Lucky was returned.

The little hedgehog was completely unafraid as he ran around, using obstacles like an assault course. The arch created by Darryl's toes touching the floor was a favourite and he ran beneath his feet several times before climbing over his calves, then charging across the room to run over a lumpy blanket that sheltered the more timid Boudicca.

This type of contact did not impress our last arrival and she expressed her disgust verbally by snorting loudly. '*Get off!*'

"The bedroom door is not the only one that Lucky has figured out," Darryl told us, as Joshua made sure the little escape artist was unable to try again.

"Oh?" I said curiously.

"I went into the cupboard to get some more blankets. When I looked down, I could see him watching me. Then a few minutes later I saw him trying to push the sliding door open with his nose."

I laughed. My opinion of hedgehogs had completely changed since we had our first guest at the hotel. I did not know what I thought a hedgehog would be like before our first resident, but within a very short time I realised that they were bright little creatures with sparkling personalities and, just like people, they were all completely individual.

Boudicca was not as involved with us as Lucky was and chose to hide under a blanket rather than take the opportunity to investigate the room beyond her cage. Boudicca's time for roaming was usually the middle of the night.

It was Joshua who heard the noise when he visited the bathroom at about 2 o'clock one morning.

He came and woke us when he heard some strange sounds coming from downstairs.

Quickly we rose and soon realised that Boudicca was missing. She had obviously discovered the loose catch keeping the lid to her cage in place and had taken the opportunity to escape.

The lock had become slack after years of use and had not been a problem with other hedgehogs, but Boudicca had proved determined to go it alone.

I witnessed this one night when I heard some noises in the 'Special Guest' room. I got up and went in to find Boudicca, arms stretched upwards, fingers and head outside of the cage, glaring at me, furious she had been caught.

"Boudicca," I said.

She lowered her head down, but continued glaring at me through the bars of her cage.

I took a step forward. "Boudicca!"

She dropped herself down and continued staring through narrowed eyes, hoping I would go away.

I stepped into the room and locked the lid. I thought it had been an accident and that we had not clicked the catch properly. We never thought further steps would be required to keep her in place – until that fateful night when she proved otherwise.

Darryl and I went downstairs, not sure about what we would find. Scraping noises, made when an animal drags their claws across a solid surface, could be clearly heard when we reached the bottom of the stairs. We began our search in the living room, then quickly moved into the dining room when it became apparent that the noise was coming from there – but we could not find her anywhere.

We looked in all the obvious places: under the sideboard, in the corners, behind the curtains. These were areas that the hedgehogs seemed to prefer, but when we had exhausted all of those possibilities, we stopped and listened to try to identify the direction of the sound.

Scraping and scratching could be heard close by, but somehow still seemed like it was at a distant location.

We looked around baffled, until suddenly Darryl dropped to his knees in front of the sideboard and peered inside one of the slots which was designed to hold bottles.

"There she is," he exclaimed triumphantly. "She's as far in as she can go, trying to dig her way through the back."

It took us some time to persuade Boudicca to come out from the small channel as she kept curling up every time we touched her. This resulted in her becoming more jammed and unable to be shifted. Each time we would have to wait for her to calm down before we could try again. Finally, we gave up trying to persuade her to back up and simply rolled her out – full-on spikes and all. Then, after a spell that took longer than we would have liked, especially at that time of night, everyone, including her, gratefully went back to bed.

From that point on, whenever we left her, there was always a heavy (hedgehog) doorstop standing guard on top of her cage to prevent any further attempts to escape.

Lucky could be trusted a little bit more than Boudicca. He was more curious and adventurous, rather than a burst for freedom. Still, he was good at opening the door, if it was not quite clicked shut, and as a result, had to be retrieved several times from the study and on one occasion was caught on his way down the stairs as I came up with a cup of tea for Darryl.

"You, mister!" I said, pointing at Lucky, who did a swift turnabout and started up the stairs again as fast as his little legs and stout body allowed.

'If I get upstairs fast enough, she'll not realise it was me.'

As spring came the days warmed up and we had some long spells of nice weather.

This allowed us to release Boudicca and Lucky quite early in the year.

Mid-April, soon after it had turned dark, Boudicca went out first as we had been aware for some time that she was unhappy being held in captivity.

They are always released into a den at the back of the garden with some mealworms nearby so they are aware of where to come to find food and shelter, if they should choose to return.

I thought that Boudicca's release would be a joyous affair – but it was not. She seemed anxious and confused by what was happening, and sniffed around nervously.

I returned to the house and cried.

My parting words of, 'Stay safe, baby,' were particularly sad, as I expected Boudicca to be overjoyed and to make good her escape as fast as she could – but she did not. We went out an hour later to check the den and she was gone.

Lucky's reaction was very different and he was completely relaxed.

Joshua was holding the torch, shining the beam into the feeding area, as Darryl popped Lucky into the den. "Do you think he was born here?" he asked, as Lucky had a very quick sniff around, then turned and went straight into the bedding area.

"He certainly looks like he knows where he is," I said.

Darryl closed the lid and we headed towards the house, leaving him to settle in.

"Stay safe, baby," I muttered.

Lucky.

Skype, when she was living with Jackie.

Two Sisters and a Witch

It was late September, when the dark nights were already starting to draw in around seven, when we acquired our first resident at 'The Hedgehog Hotel'. This was surprisingly early, but was about right for when the late season babies would have just left their mums.

Hoglets have their eyes closed until they are about two weeks old. At about four weeks old they will start to go out, hunting for food, and learn what they can eat from their mothers. They will usually be no more than six weeks old by the time they leave and go out into the world on their own.

Therefore, it was that time, late September, when Darryl went off for a walk, and one went out and two came back.

A tiny little hedgehog that must have left mum within the week had been seen hanging around the hotel waiting to be noticed.

She was particularly small and without even weighing her we knew that she would never put on enough weight to survive the winter.

The next day our second resident arrived. She had also been seen hanging around the front garden and again was obviously too small for hibernation.

"Do you think they might be sisters?" Joshua asked Darryl as he brought the tiny hedgehog, that fitted easily in his hand, into the living room.

"Could be. Hedgehogs often have at least two hoglets in a litter. We'll see how they are together." He passed the little creature to Joshua, who put her into the same cage. "If they're fine, we'll leave them overnight and see how it goes."

The moment the two hedgehogs saw each other, they hurried together and began to rub faces.

Joshua smiled. "It looks like a family reunion."

"What do you want to call them?" Darryl asked.

"I think it will have to be Sugar and Spice."

Thankfully, Sugar and Spice got along a bit better than Holly and Poppy. The only squabbling seemed to be over who got the most blankets, which worked out to be just as well as our third resident at the hotel arrived a month later after I spotted her in the back garden early one evening nearer to Halloween.

Her initial name of Lamia, the queen witch in the film *Stardust*, was chosen by Darryl, but we kept forgetting what she was called, so we changed it to the title of the film instead.

The autumn was mild, so we were happy to move all three into the two guinea pig cages in the garage.

Sugar and Spice were housed together. They seemed to be happy to share blankets so Darryl put them both at one end of the cage so they could snuggle up.

Stardust was in the other cage, with an additional blanket to ward off the cold instead.

Everything seemed to be going fine and the twice-daily clean outs became routine for everyone involved until one day, in mid-January, Joshua began to notice a change in Sugar's behaviour. Over the period of a few days she became sweet by name, but not by nature.

Initially, he noticed there was a little bit of squabbling between the two sisters. "They seem to be jostling over blankets." He looked at Darryl. "Do you think we should give them their own bedding?"

Darryl began rummaging in a box. "It might be a good idea to put them at opposite ends of the cage from each other." He retrieved a number of blankets, then set up separate bedding areas for the sisters.

This seemed to help, certainly for Spice, but things went from bad to worse with Sugar.

"She seems to be getting grumpier by the day," Joshua said, puzzled, as he quickly put Sugar down in the puppy run. "Soon after I picked her up, I felt a wet nose on my finger. For a few seconds she sniffed at my hand, then suddenly the little horror tried to bite me." He showed me the digit. There were a number of tiny red indentations in the soft flesh near the nail.

"Are you alright?" I asked, concerned.

He nodded. "She didn't break the skin, just gave me a fright."

"That's not like her. So far she's lived up to her name." I looked into the puppy run, where Spice ran around like a little steam train, sniffing the sides and examining every inch of the floor, whilst Sugar tried to shuffle under a blanket which had been added in case they wanted to hide.

"I'm also not sure if she's eating very much. If at all," Joshua said.

"Oh?"

"We were putting twice as much food into the cage for the two of them, then suddenly quite a bit of it is left in the morning."

"If she doesn't improve, we'll get her checked out."

We finished cleaning, then returned them to their cages and left them alone for the night.

The following day the morning clean out had barely begun, when Darryl called us outside.

We hurried to see what was going on, then stood amazed by a sight we had not seen before.

"What is she doing?" I asked.

"She's hibernating," Darryl said.

Joshua dropped to his knees to examine the hedgehog more closely. "Are you sure?"

The blankets were pulled back to reveal a full ball of impenetrable spines.

"Yes," Darryl replied. "I was warned about it."

Joshua looked up. "None of the others have ever hibernated. Why should Sugar?"

"I don't know," Darryl confessed. "I can only think it's because the garage is colder than the house."

"There was a sudden cold spell last week, which is when she started to become grumpy," Joshua pointed out.

"Well there you go," I said. "It's just surprising it hasn't affected the others." I bent down, picked up a bundle of dirty blankets and was just about to move away, heading for the washer, when suddenly Darryl stopped me.

"Oh no! She's done it again," I groaned.

"What's wrong?" Joshua asked.

Darryl pointed into the freshly prepared cage where Stardust had just been put to bed.

"Oh!"

There she was, standing in the middle of a clean blanket, looking up at us completely unafraid, and just behind her was a rather large deposit of poo.

"No matter how long I leave it," Darryl moaned, "she just seems to like dirtying in a clean blanket."

Stardust was quite a size now and could have easily been released into the wild, if the weather had not been so cold.

"Never mind," I said, "give me that one as well and that'll be a full load for the washer."

Stardust's habit of dirtying in her bedding became a bit of a problem over the next few weeks when the weather took a turn for the worse and she became even more reluctant to leave the toasty warmth of her blankets. This resulted in her being rather more smelly than usual.

Joshua wrinkled his nose. "Phew! She stinks," he said, a few days into the cold spell.

A pungent aroma of urine rose from Stardust as she was transferred to the puppy run.

"I think we'd better give her a bath," I suggested.

Joshua's eyes widened. "A bath?"

"Well not quite a bath," I smiled, "more like a sink."

I lifted her from the puppy run and took her upstairs.

Joshua followed behind. "Won't she get upset?" he asked.

"Hedgehogs are good swimmers in the wild and can often pass quite happily across small areas of water. It's only if they can't get out that they get into difficulties. Garden ponds need to have stones or steps to help them to escape, otherwise they're in danger of drowning, but as long as they can climb out, then they are usually OK."

We arrived in the bathroom.

"What shall we bathe her with?" Joshua asked.

"Baby shampoo, because if the soap gets in her eyes it won't sting."

We filled the sink a quarter full with slightly warm water, with a good squirt of shampoo, then added the hedgehog to the mix.

To our amazement Stardust was as sweet and relaxed as ever and seemed completely unfazed. In fact, she almost seemed to enjoy the water being gently splashed over her spines. The only time she made any attempt to curl up, and even then it was only a half-hearted effort, was when some stray droplets accidentally landed in her eyes.

A few minutes later, when she smelled slightly more flowery and a lot less like a urine-soaked hedgehog, we rinsed her and gently wrapped her in a towel.

"Hello!"

"We're in the bathroom," I called to Darryl.

Quickly, he hurried upstairs then stopped abruptly in the doorway. "What's been going on here?" he asked, smiling widely at Stardust's little face peeking out from a small hole in a wrap of fluffy orange towel.

"She was a bit smelly so we gave her a wash," Joshua informed him.

"Well I don't know how much she enjoyed it," Darryl laughed, "but she certainly seems to be enjoying the towel dry afterwards."

Sugar stayed in hibernation for about six weeks, then suddenly one day she woke up.

During her spell of sleeping, so deeply she was at a near death rate, she never ate and her heart rate dropped from about two hundred and forty beats per minute down to about six. Her body temperature also fell from thirty-four degrees to about five. This allowed her to preserve energy whilst she used up her body's fat reserves throughout the hibernation period.

"I found her awake," Joshua said, holding Sugar up for me to see, "and she's obviously very hungry this morning as all of the food is completely gone."

A juicy black nose shot forward, her spines flattened against her neck, as Sugar stretched her head out, sniffing at my face. *"Hellooo. I feel sooo much better now."*

As spring approached, we began to think about when the best time would be to release the hedgehogs. As before, we decided a spell in the garden to get them used to the smells and temperatures of the outside world again would be a good idea.

We tried them on the grass like Horace, who turned out to be Harriet, but quickly found the sisters could not be trusted to just wander around the garden untethered.

A slow, *'I'm not really going anywhere,'* crawl towards the conifers, under our beady gaze, quickly become a mad dash of, *'Run!'* as they neared the trees, before being swiftly rounded up and returned to the middle of the garden. After a couple of episodes of this, we gave up and put them outside in the puppy run for half an hour every day instead.

Stardust, on the other hand, was so chilled, she could be trusted to just wander around the grass until we were ready to bring her in.

It was a beautiful spring day and Joshua was watching her hanging out with the cats in the sun.

The garden had begun a transformation from death to life. The bleakness of winter was being washed away in a flurry of buds, flowers, baby birds and the heady aroma of wild garlic wafting from the shrubs at the back.

All the animals, plus one child, were outside and as I went to see how everybody was doing, I heard Joshua laughing as I neared the back door.

I stepped into the garden. "What's wrong?"

He pointed at Stardust.

I looked down to find the hedgehog, head shoved between the drainpipe and the house, pushing for all she was worth.

'If I push hard enough, I'll definitely get through the gap.'

"She's happy to chill and hang out with the cats, but then every now and again she decides she wants to move the house. I've had to shift her three times already in the last fifteen minutes."

"Well it looks like we'll have to do it again," I said, as I bent down and moved the hedgehog back onto the path.

Stardust finally gave up trying to move the house after a few days, which was a great relief as I was worried she might get stuck somewhere when she was released.

A week later, when we were happy they were ready, all three hedgehogs were returned to the wild.

"Stay safe, baby!" I muttered, as I hurried indoors.

Sugar and Spice.

Lucy chilling in the garden with Stardust.

Isabel the Magnificent

There were only a few times where we had one hedgehog residing at the hotel over the winter. On one of those occasions, it was probably just as well – like the year we had Isabel the Magnificent, or Izzy for short.

Izzy did not start out as Isabel the Magnificent, in fact she was Isabel the rat, Isabel the horror, Isabel the strop, but as she grew things began to change – not always for the better.

She was a late season baby who was too small to hibernate and was spotted in the front garden of No. 2 Honey Bee Street in early November by Darryl as he returned from one of his walks.

Even though it was late I was thankfully still up, so we did not end up with a hedgehog on the bed on that occasion.

I helped him set up a cage and we settled her down for the night.

The temperature had plunged that day so we decided it would probably be a good idea to move Izzy into the 'Special Guest' room until the weather warmed up – which, as it happened, turned out to be April.

I was always reluctant to have a hedgehog inside the house as they could often be quite smelly. Whether they pooed in their bedding, which a lot of them often did, or were very clean and had a poo corner. Either way you had the smell, which was sometimes reluctant to stay in one room no matter how hard you tried. It also resulted in us losing the spare bedroom for, what could be, up to six months of the year. Either way, the well-being of the hedgehog was our main priority, so in this case it was important that she moved into the house to make sure she stayed safe.

Within days we knew that Izzy had a strong personality and she asserted herself pretty much from the start.

Not long into her stay Darryl discovered an aspect of the hedgehog's persona, which up until then, we had never encountered before.

Ever since we nearly lost Harriet, the hedgehogs who stayed at the hotel were regularly weighed to make sure they were gaining, rather than losing weight.

This is even more important when they are very small as they can rapidly lose weight and over a matter of days this can become life-threatening.

There are various things that can cause this problem, such as worms, which a simple treatment can resolve. It can also be due to the hedgehog not being warm enough. They do like to be surprisingly warm and often will not eat if they are chilly as this can start to trigger their hibernation process. Either way, when they are tiny even a small amount of weight loss can be dangerous and needs to be urgently addressed by a hedgehog expert.

It was early one morning, a few weeks into her stay, that Darryl was carrying Izzy downstairs for her daily weighing and it was then that she decided to start to become awkward.

By now, we had had so many hedgehogs staying at the hotel, Darryl was so used to carrying them that he no longer needed to use a towel or blanket to handle them, unless they were nervous or in a bad mood.

On this particular morning he was carrying Izzy downstairs, both hands scooped underneath her tummy, but when he got half way to the bottom he suddenly stopped.

I was in the kitchen, preparing her food and waiting for the hotel's latest resident to arrive when I heard him calling, "Stop it, Izzy!"

I hurried to see what was going on, to find Darryl struggling to keep the hedgehog safely in his hands.

Izzy was rocking herself from side to side, her spines raised, making it uncomfortable for Darryl to carry her. This deliberate and conscious act on the hedgehog's part became obvious when I reached out to help him, just as Izzy began to slip.

At this point you would have expected her spines to completely raise and for her to curl up into a ball. Instead, quite the opposite happened when suddenly her spines dropped, flattening against her body.

Quickly, I grabbed a blanket and Darryl passed her over. He examined his hands. "That was deliberate," he said, annoyed. "She was deliberately making it difficult for me to carry her, but once she thought she was going to fall, suddenly she flattened her spines so that she was no longer spiking me."

That was the first of a number of devious acts on Izzy's part over the next few months, which made us realise that she was not best pleased whenever she had to interact with us.

I was the next to fall victim to Izzy's prickly personality when I was watching her on the floor whilst waiting for her cage to be cleaned.

Some of our hedgehogs quite liked to be stroked and would flatten their spines against their bodies when you ran your hand over their backs or sides. Others quite liked a massage, which Joshua discovered when we had a hedgehog called Amber.

One night she was sitting quietly on his knee whilst waiting to return to her cage. When she tried to wander off, he touched her on the back of the neck to stop her and realised that she liked the contact when she flattened her body across his thighs.

Gently he rubbed the large muscle running over her shoulders and her body relaxed further, flattening even more across his legs.

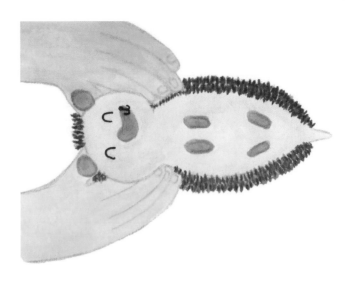

Nightly massages became a regular thing for Amber, who understandably was one of our most chilled hedgehogs to stay at the hotel.

Another, less chilled hedgehog, we called Blossom, also liked as little to do with us as possible, but wanted her feet massaging. She would lower her face down so that it was hidden and her head spines were up. At the same time she would drop her feet, pushing them as far below your hand as possible so that she could get the soft, leathery pad behind her toes gently massaged.

That day, on the floor, when I was watching Izzy, as I waited for her cage to be cleaned, I thought I had discovered that she liked to be stroked along her side also.

I was kneeling on the floor, when she came up and pushed herself against my leg, rubbing her side, with some force, along the length of my calf. When she reached my ankle, I felt a wet nose sniffing my bare toes. I moved her back to my knee and again she rubbed against my leg until she once more arrived at my ankle. Again, I felt the wet nose very briefly on my toes – then moments later she bit me. This was no defence mechanism, it was pure malice.

She turned out to be a bit of a biter as Darryl discovered when he was getting ready to put her back into her cage the following week and he thought he saw a parasite living on her face.

We are often asked about fleas whenever we mention we are hedgehog carers, but fleas were a problem that we never encountered. The usual parasite the hedgehogs arrived with were ticks. Most of the time it was just the odd one, but sometimes they arrived quite badly infested and we had to remove thirty or more ticks from at least one hedgehog. When the ticks were large, they were easily spotted and removed, but sometimes they were too small to be located and it was not until they had grown to a certain size before they became obvious and we were able to get them off safely. Removing them was always Darryl's dubious honour – because he liked it.

Izzy did not appear to have any ticks when she first came into the hotel, but after she had been with us for about a month Darryl thought he noticed one on her face, as he was about to put her back to bed. He held her up, looking at the soft fur running around the top of her eye, where there appeared to be a small white blemish, which can often be the sign of a tick. He moved her closer to get a better look, then suddenly she leaned forward and bit him on the end of his nose – and there she hung on, refusing to budge.

"Ow, Izzy, that hurts," Darryl stated, moving her slightly back in the hope she would release him. Far from it, as instead Izzy continued to hang on, her sharp little teeth piercing Darryl's skin. Then worse, suddenly she started ratting, shaking her head rapidly from side to side as if she were trying to break off a piece.

"Ow, Izzy! Ow!" Darryl squeaked. "That's not nice." Desperate to extract her from his nose, he moved her back again and much to his relief, this time she let go.

As time went on and the older she got, Izzy's behaviour became more and more outrageous. Then, when she was in the equivalent of her teens, around about six months old, she became quite the little strop.

She became increasingly difficult when she had to be picked up. She would snort and grunt, then try her best to spike us by jumping up whenever a hand came close. A towel became a must as eventually this was the only way to safely extract her from her cage.

She also became difficult at feeding times and Joshua used to make us laugh with his impression of her.

His nose raised, his eyes closed, he would hold up a hand, palm out and turn his face slightly away. "Just leave the food and go," he said quickly. He extended his arm, raising the palm towards my face. "Just go, I say!"

She had been with us about five months and by then we definitely got the impression that Izzy was getting fed up with being held in captivity – even if it was for her own good. Her increasing weight was also becoming a worry and as a result we were very keen to get her out.

Hedgehogs instinctively eat so that they can put on as much weight as possible to be able to safely hibernate. Therefore, it can be difficult to keep a captive hedgehog's weight under control. Often if there is an attempt to put them on a diet or even to cut back on their food, they will eat anything they can.

This was the case with Izzy. One day after her weight hit eight hundred grams, we decided to cut back on her food. The following morning when Joshua went in to clean her out, he was shocked to discover she had newspapers in her mouth.

We were desperate to stop her gaining more weight, but were stuck with the dilemma of Izzy eating anything if she felt she was not getting enough food.

It was decided that more time in the puppy run was the best solution, but as the problem with releasing her was cold wet weather, we could not put the enclosure outside.

Another problem began to emerge, as by now Izzy was also showing worrying signs of depression and seemed to have almost given up any hope of being released. She looked at us sadly and the fighting spirit that had defined her was gone.

We watched the forecast closely, eager for a decent spell of dry settled weather. Then around about mid-May, with great relief, the weather cleared.

That night the whole family gathered to release Izzy back into the wild, after a mammoth six months' stay at the hotel.

Joshua put her down, pointing her nose at the den, but the moment he released her, instead of going inside she turned right and stomped off, heading towards the back of the garden.

'You lot better stay away from me!' *Stomp, stomp, stomp. 'Our paths had better not cross again.' Stomp, stomp, stomp. 'You'd better hope you never run into me.'*

We all stood flabbergasted by the hedgehog strop and instead of my usual cry of, 'Stay safe, baby,' this time I called, sarcastically, "Thank you, Izzy," as she did a full-on teenage strop and stormed out of the garden.

Three Years Later

Joshua pointed outside. "There's a hedgehog in the garden." He looked at me. "What do you think? Should we bring it in?"

"I know it's December, but it has been mild and we have been putting food out regularly for any visitors." I thought a moment. "Bring it in and we'll check its weight and make sure it has no injuries then, if it's fine, we'll put it back outside."

Joshua dashed out, carrying a small towel to safely pick up the hedgehog, then a short while later I could see without the need for weighing that it was definitely a healthy size for hibernation.

Checking it for injuries was a little bit more difficult as the hedgehog kept its face down and the head spines pointing forward. Still, I could see its legs and it was then that I thought I might possibly know this hedgehog.

"I'll bet that's Izzy," I said. "Isabel. Isabel!" I called.

Izzy was always a big girl, even without the weight, as fully grown, even her legs had been chunky. She was always going to be a large hedgehog, no matter what we did.

I had barely finished speaking her name, when out popped her face and nose twitching, she looked around the kitchen.

'I know you. I know this place.'

"It is you, sweetie," I smiled. "Look at you! You're magnificent!"

Izzy never curled up again and was instantly relaxed with us. Her years in the wild had made her realise that we were not axe murderers after all and had only been looking after her best interests. In fact we were probably the best thing that ever happened to her.

Quickly, I prepared her some food, before we put her and the crunchies in the den at the back of the garden.

All the way to the house we could hear her chomping, crunching on the biscuits and

to our delight she hibernated in the garden
that winter.

Isabel the Magnificent in a strop.

A Final Thought on the Matter

We have been fortunate enough to help save the lives of at least twenty-one hedgehogs over a period of about fifteen years. Along with this honour we have also been delighted to get to know these amazing little creatures and to observe their fantastic personalities first hand.

We have been so lucky to be a part of helping to preserve the species and although it pains us every time we release a hedgehog, for fear of what might happen to them, we know that their place is in the wild. This is where they thrive and, hopefully, go on to produce more little hoglets to ensure their future is secure.

Goodbye!

Printed in Great Britain
by Amazon

78838480R00083